Nowhere
Like Home

SCHOLASTIC

MARVEL

Scholastic Children's Books
Euston House,
24 Eversholt Street,
London NW1 1DB, UK

A division of Scholastic Ltd
London ~ New York ~ Toronto ~ Sydney ~ Auckland
Mexico City ~ New Delhi ~ Hong Kong

This book was first published in Australia in 2016 by Scholastic Australia
Published in the UK by Scholastic Ltd, 2017

ISBN 978 1 40717 376 4

Printed in Malaysia

2 4 6 8 10 9 7 5 3 1

Papers used by Scholastic Children's Books are made from woods grown in sustainable forests.

www.scholastic.co.uk

MARVEL
GUARDIANS OF THE GALAXY

LEVEL 2

Nowhere Like Home

Adapted from **Knowhere to Run**, *written by* **Chris 'Doc' Wyatt**
Illustrated by **Ron Lim** *and* **Andy Troy**

MARVEL
Los Angeles
New York

Peter was once a little boy
on planet Earth.
He liked to play outside
and read books about space.

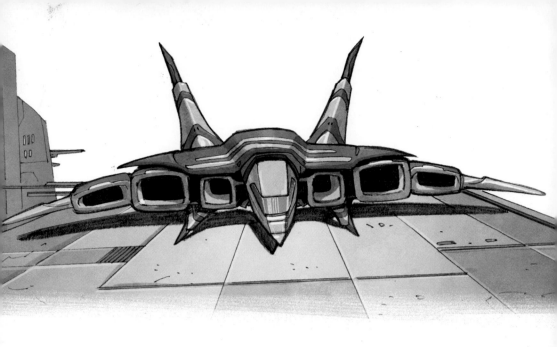

Now Peter is Star-Lord, a Super Hero.
He has a spaceship and helps to
protect the galaxy.

Star-Lord lives on a space station
called Knowhere.

He is on a Super Hero team.
They are the Guardians
of the Galaxy.

One day, Star-Lord feels sad.

He misses Earth.

A game will make him feel better.

He will go and play darts with Rocket.

Rocket has special darts.
"They will always go where you
tell them to go," says Rocket.

8

They have fun playing.
But Star-Lord cannot stop thinking
about Earth.

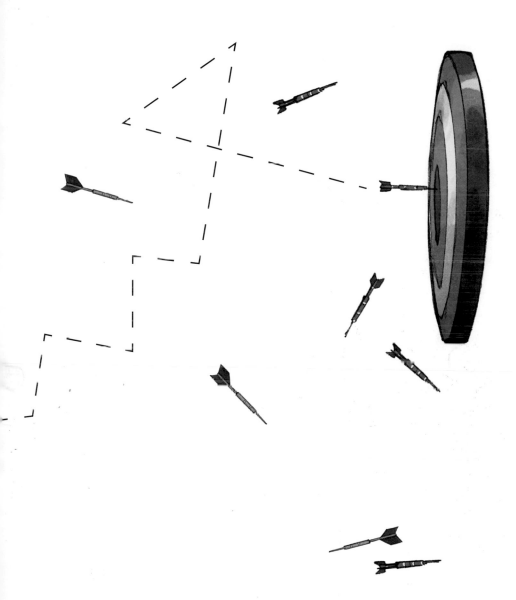

Later that day, Cosmo visits Star-Lord.
Cosmo is a talking dog from Earth.
He is the boss of security on Knowhere.
"Hi Cosmo, what's up?" asks Star-Lord.

"A hero from Earth is here," says Cosmo.
"Is Earth in trouble?" asks Star-Lord.
"Maybe," replies Cosmo.

The hero is Captain Marvel.
She needs help.
Some aliens are making bombs.
They are hiding on Knowhere.

"The aliens will use the bombs to destroy the Earth," explains Captain Marvel.

"We must stop them," says Star-Lord. Cosmo's deputy, Yon-Rogg, will help the heroes.

The other Guardians of the Galaxy
want to help too.
But Star-Lord keeps the plan secret.
If spies hear the plan,
it may not work.

Gamora, Drax, Rocket and Groot
follow Star-Lord.
They will help him no matter what.

Groot sees Star-Lord with
Yon-Rogg and Captain Marvel.
"I am Groot!" he says.

Yon-Rogg takes the heroes to a secret place.

They can see aliens
with a box full of bombs.
There is no time to waste!

Star-Lord kicks the door open.
They rush into the room.
The aliens fight back!

Star-Lord and Yon-Rogg are trapped.
An alien is holding a bomb.
"This bomb will destroy you," he says.
He throws the bomb at Captain Marvel!

"Stop that bomb!" Yon-Rogg yells.
Star-Lord thinks fast.
He has one of Rocket's special darts.

The dart will go
where Star-Lord tells it to go.
"Go to the bomb!" he says.

The dart hits the bomb.
The bomb crashes into the box.
It destroys all the other bombs!

Captain Marvel is saved!
She runs over to free Star-Lord
and Yon-Rogg.

The aliens lose the battle!
Yon-Rogg takes them away.
"Good job," Cosmo tells Star-Lord
and Captain Marvel.

But then Rocket, Drax, Groot and
Gamora arrive.

They are in a hurry.

"Look out!" cries Gamora. "The battle
is not over yet!"

It is the alien boss!
He is angry that the bombs
are destroyed.
He attacks Star-Lord and Cosmo.

"Do not mess with our friend!"
Rocket yells.
Star-Lord's team protect him.
They defeat the alien boss!

Captain Marvel is going home.
"Do you want to come back to Earth
with me?" she asks Star-Lord.
"No, thanks. My home is here now,"
Star-Lord replies.

Captain Marvel flies back to Earth.
The Guardians wave goodbye.

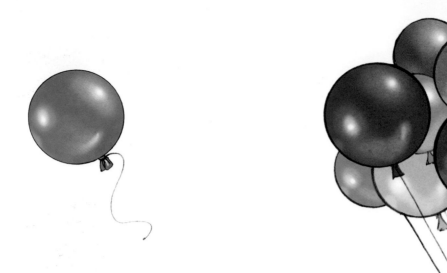

The next day, Cosmo has a surprise.
"It is your Earth birthday!" he says.

"Really?" says Star-Lord. "Wow!"
His team gives him a cake!

The Guardians of the Galaxy
take Star-Lord out for his birthday.

Star-Lord is happy to be with his friends.
He will never forget Earth.
But there is Knowhere like home!